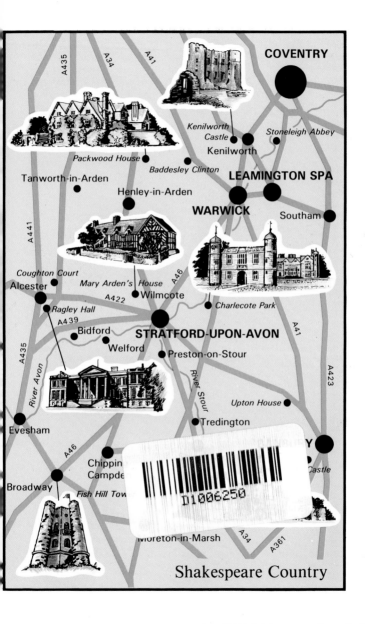

COVENTRY

Kenilworth Castle

Stoneleigh Abbey

Kenilworth

Packwood House

Baddesley Clinton

Tanworth-in-Arden

LEAMINGTON SPA

Henley-in-Arden

WARWICK

Southam

Coughton Court

Alcester

Mary Arden's House

Wilmcote

Charlecote Park

Ragley Hall

A439

Bidford

STRATFORD-UPON-AVON

Welford

Preston-on-Stour

River Avon

River Stour

Upton House

Evesham

Tredington

Castle

Chipping
Campde

D1006250

Broadway

Fish Hill Tow

Moreton-in-Marsh

Shakespeare Country

The whole world has heard of William Shakespeare, poet and playwright, and of his birthplace, Stratford-upon-Avon. Stratford is Warwickshire's oldest market town, and it is at the heart of Shakespeare Country, which stretches for twenty miles in all directions.

This is one of the most beautiful parts of England. There are gently rolling fields, scattered woods, parks and orchards, small unspoiled villages, and towns with a long history – Shakespeare Country, surprisingly little changed from the time the poet knew and loved it, four centuries ago.

Acknowledgments:
The Droeshout engraving of Shakespeare from the First Folio of 1623 used on the cover and on the title page is reproduced by permission of the Shakespeare Birthplace Trust, Stratford-upon-Avon; the maps on the front endpaper are by Graham Marlow, who is also responsible for the design of the book.

The photograph on page 43 is from Aerofilms Library; photographs on pages 9 (top), 12, 13, 15, 18, 19 (top), 21 (2), 22, 23, 34 (top), 35 (top), 36, 37 (top), 44 (bottom), 48, and 49 (top) are from Britain on View; pages 28 and 30 are from Mary Campbell Photographs, Warwick; page 47 (top) is by Elspeth Crichton; pages 5 (top) and 9 (bottom) are from Robert Harding Picture Library; cover photograph and pages 4, 5 (bottom), 8, 11, 19 (bottom), 20, 24, 25, 26 (2), 27 (2), 30/31, 32 (2), 34 (bottom), 35 (bottom), 41 (top), 44 (top), 46, 47 (bottom), and 49 (bottom) are all reproduced by courtesy of the Heart of England Tourist Board; pages 33, and 51 (2) are from Jarrold & Sons Ltd; pages 38/9 (3) are by permission of the National Trust; page 29 is from Warwick Castle Ltd; back cover and pages 6 (2), 7 (2), 10/11, 14, 16 (2), 17 (3), 37, 40 (2), 41 (bottom), 42 (2), 45 (2), and 50 (3) are by Chris Wright Photography.

British Library Cataloguing in Publication Data

Fox, Levi
    Discovering Shakespeare country.—
    (A Ladybird book. Series 861; v. 3).
    1. Stratford-upon-Avon Region (Warwickshire)
    —Description and travel—Juvenile literature
    I. Title
    914.24'89   DA690.S92
    ISBN 0-7214-1003-0

First edition

Published by Ladybird Books Ltd Loughborough Leicestershire UK
Ladybird Books Inc Lewiston Maine 04240 USA

© LADYBIRD BOOKS LTD MCMLXXXVII

Printed in England

DISCOVERING
Shakespeare Country

written by
Dr LEVI FOX
OBE, DL, MA

Ladybird Books

The best place to start exploring Shakespeare Country is Stratford-upon-Avon itself. It began as a settlement beside a ford across the River Avon, and it has a fascinating history.

River Avon, looking towards the Shakespeare Memorial Theatre

In early times Roman and Anglo-Saxon invaders travelled along the Avon valley and settled on sites a little distance from Clopton Bridge. This was built later, about five hundred years ago, by Sir Hugh Clopton, a native of Stratford who became Lord Mayor of London, and it is a fine bridge.

Clopton Bridge

Holy Trinity Church

By the eleventh century, when the Domesday Survey was compiled, a small community of people had established themselves at Stratford, tilling the soil and grinding their corn at a mill near the church.

Soon afterwards they were given the right to hold a market and fairs. This meant that Stratford could develop as a place where farm produce and stock from the surrounding countryside was bought and sold.

By the time Shakespeare was born in 1564 the pattern of the town's central streets already existed and so did their names, which still remain today. A traveller who visited

Pig roast at the annual Mop Fair, Stratford-upon-Avon

6

Mason's Court

Stratford in the sixteenth century was struck by its 'very large streets' and its buildings which were 'reasonably well builded of timber'.

Many of those buildings, such as Mason's Court in Rother Street and Harvard House in High Street, re-built after a fire in 1596, still survive. Harvard House was the home of Katherine Rogers, mother of John Harvard, who founded the American university which bears his name.

Harvard House

Shakespeare's Birthplace

William Shakespeare was the son of John Shakespeare, a glover and wool dealer who held various public offices and became Bailiff of the town in 1568. He lived in Henley Street in the house preserved as Shakespeare's Birthplace, which is visited by about a million people each year, from all over the world.

It is a half-timbered building dating back to the sixteenth century. The part which the Shakespeare family lived in is furnished in the style of a middle-class tradesman. The traditional birthroom is on the first floor, and there is a display of books, manuscripts, pictures and other items

The room where Shakespeare was born

illustrating the life, times and works of Shakespeare in the museum part of the building.

The garden is of special interest. It is planted with trees, herbs and flowers mentioned in Shakespeare's writings.

The Gower Memorial to Shakespeare

The Shakespeare Centre, Stratford-upon-Avon

In contrast to the Birthplace, the Shakespeare Centre which overlooks the garden is a modern building of striking design.

It is the headquarters of the Shakespeare Birthplace Trust. The Trust looks after the Shakespearian properties which are national memorials and also has a specialised Shakespearian library.

Stratford's medieval guild buildings in Church Street

are among the most picturesque of their kind.

King Edward VI Grammar School, where Shakespeare was educated, still exists, and its original buildings are still used. The half-timbered school room occupies the first floor of the Guildhall built in 1416 and 1418.

The school also uses the Guild Chapel, which is alongside. It was built by the Guild of the Holy Cross, founded in 1269. Over the chancel arch is a famous wall painting of the last day of judgement.

King Edward VI Grammar School, where Shakespeare was educated

The garden at New Place

Opposite the Guild Chapel on the corner of Chapel Street, New Place once stood. It was a large house where Shakespeare lived in retirement after his busy working life in London. He died there in 1616.

New Place was demolished in 1759 and only the foundations now remain, in a garden setting. The Elizabethan Knott garden and the Great Garden of New Place nearby were both once part of Shakespeare's home. Here may be seen an ancient mulberry tree which is said to have been grown from a cutting of a tree planted by Shakespeare himself.

The house at the side of New Place belonged to Thomas Nash, the first husband of Shakespeare's grand-daughter, Elizabeth Hall. It is now used as a local history museum.

The half-timbered Shakespeare and Falcon Hotels are also in Chapel Street.

Another fine example of an Elizabethan house is Hall's Croft in Old Town. This was the home of Shakespeare's daughter Susanna and her husband, John Hall, who was a well-known doctor in Stratford.

Dr Hall's casebook still survives. It has some fascinating details about his patients and their ailments and cures.

Hall's Croft, the home of Shakespeare's son-in-law, Dr John Hall

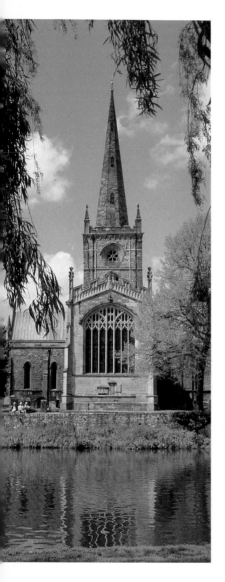

Holy Trinity Church, where Shakespeare was baptised and buried

Old Town leads to the Church of Holy Trinity, on the banks of the Avon. Shakespeare was baptised and buried here, and people have been coming to see his grave and monument from within a few years of his death.

In its own right, however, Holy Trinity is a particularly beautiful church. Some parts of it date from the twelfth century. Some of the things you should see: the medieval sanctuary door knocker and the fine series of carved misericords in the chancel; the Clopton Chapel and its monuments; and the old font and chained Bible.

Inside Holy Trinity Church – the monument to Shakespeare

IVDICIO PYLIVM, GENIO SOCRATEM, ARTE MARONEM,
TERRA TEGIT, POPVLVS MÆRET, OLYMPVS HABET

STAY PASSENGER, WHY GOEST THOV BY SO FAST,
READ IF THOV CANST, WHOM ENVIOVS DEATH HATH PLAST,
WITH IN THIS MONVMENT SHAKSPEARE: WITH WHOME,
QVICK NATVRE DIDE: WHOSE NAME, DOTH DECK Y.ᵉ TOMBE,
FAR MORE, THEN COST: SIEH ALL, Y.ᵗ HE HATH WRITT,
LEAVES LIVING ART, BVT PAGE, TO SERVE HIS WITT.

OBIIT AÑO DO.¹ 1616
ÆTATIS 53 DIE 23 AP.

The Royal Shakespeare Theatre

The Swan Theatre

A little distance upstream from Holy Trinity Church is the Royal Shakespeare Theatre, built in 1932. It is the home of the world-famous Royal Shakespeare Company.

The Swan Theatre, opened in 1986, forms part of the theatre complex next to the Picture Gallery. Its design is based on the Elizabethan playhouse.

The cattle market

Apart from the tourists, Stratford-upon-Avon has a busy life of its own as a market town. Every Friday it has an open air market, and on Tuesdays farmers come to buy and sell their stock at the cattle market.

The town also has a number of light engineering industries.

The weekly market

Just as Shakespeare's Birthplace does, Anne Hathaway's Cottage at Shottery, about a mile from the centre of the town, attracts visitors from all over the world. Shakespeare's wife Anne Hathaway lived here before her marriage.

The Cottage is an example of one of the earliest methods used in house building in this country: oak curved timbers or 'crucks', pegged together at the top. The kitchen still has its bake-oven intact and the living room its original panelling and open chimney hearth. The famous Hathaway bed that has been there since Shakespeare's time is upstairs. Descendants of the Hathaway family lived here down to 1892 and most of the furnishings in the Cottage belonged to them.

The Cottage has an old-fashioned garden and orchard, with an unusual medley of trees, flowers and herbs.

Anne Hathaway's Cottage, Shottery

The kitchen

The living room

With Stratford as a base, where is the best place to start exploring?

First, to Wilmcote, about three miles away. You can take the route along the Ridgeway (formerly a farm track) off the Alcester road, or walk along the tow path of the canal from the town.

Mary Arden's House at Wilmcote is a magnificent sixteenth-century farmstead. It was the home of

Mary Arden's House, Wilmco

Farming tools of the past

Gipsy caravans

Shakespeare's mother, Mary Arden. The farm was still being worked as recently as 1930.

The farmhouse, with its period furniture, gives an excellent idea of domestic life in Tudor England. The barns and farm buildings house a collection of old agricultural implements, and you can also see a stone-built dovecote and a cider mill.

The Glebe Farm adjoining Mary Arden's House is also open to the public. The oldest part of this dates to the sixteenth century, but the farmhouse is now furnished in the style of the Victorian and Edwardian period. There are displays of country crafts to be seen as well, in buildings round the farmyard.

On the River Alne the pretty village of Aston Cantlow, a short distance beyond Wilmcote, has a timber-framed Guild House.

It also has an early medieval church where Shakespeare's parents are said to have been married.

Alcester

A few miles away is the small market town of Alcester.
It is of Roman origin, but possesses buildings of many
periods, and old-fashioned shops. It has a medieval
church and a seventeenth-century town hall. There are
very fine Tudor buildings in Malt Mill Lane.

23

Nearby is Coughton Court, now a National Trust property. It is the home of the Catholic family of Throckmorton and was closely associated with the Gunpowder Plot conspiracy.

Ragley Hall, built in 1690, with later additions in the early nineteenth century

Ragley Hall is a splendid classical stately home set in a spacious park just outside Alcester. It is the family home of the Marquess and Marchioness of Hertford. Anyone who likes nature trails can find one of the best here.

Main street, Henley-in-Arden

North of Wilmcote used to be well wooded: the Forest of Arden, which produced the timber used for buildings in Stratford for several centuries. Shakespeare made it the setting for his play, *As You Like It*. He must have known this part of the country very well as a boy.

Henley-in-Arden, eight miles to the north-west of Stratford on the main road to Birmingham, is an attractive old market town. It has a picturesque medieval half-timbered Guildhall and a wealth of brick and timber-framed buildings set along its main street.

The Guildhall, Henley-in-Arden

Several stately homes can be easily reached from here. Packwood House lies north of Hockley Heath, and is well worth a visit. It is a National Trust property which houses a valuable collection of

Packwood House

tapestry, needlework and furniture. The fine topiary garden in a layout symbolic of the Sermon on the Mount was planted about 1650. There are twelve yews representing Apostles, four larger ones representing Evangelists and an enormous yew representing Christ.

Baddesley Clinton is Warwickshire's unique example of a moated manor, and is very beautiful. It was the home of the Ferrers family for nearly five hundred years, and contains a great many things of historical interest.

Baddesley Clinton

The main road leads back to Warwick, central to the history of Shakespeare's Country. For centuries it has served as the county town, with its imposing Shire Hall in Northgate Street. It is a town of character and quality in its own right, preserving interesting links with its historic past.

Warwick Castle, perched alongside the River Avon, ranks high among the historic treasures of England. Formerly the home of the Earls of Warwick, whose ancestors vitally influenced the course of medieval history, the castle is at once a medieval fortress and an elegant seventeenth-century residence.

The Great Hall, Warwick Castle

Warwick Castle

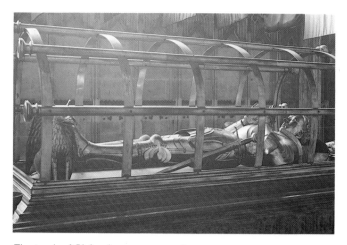

The tomb of Richard
Beauchamp, Earl of Warwick
in St Mary's Church,
Warwick

In St Mary's Church at
Warwick, re-built after a
fire which destroyed
much of the town in
1696, may be seen the
fifteenth-century
Beauchamp Chapel. It
contains the famous
effigy of Richard
Beauchamp, Earl of
Warwick.

Another of Warwick's
treasures is Lord
Leycester's Hospital,

which stands by the West Gate, itself a reminder that Warwick was once a walled town.

The Hospital was founded by Robert Dudley, Earl of Leicester, the favourite of Queen Elizabeth I, as an almshouse for 'soldiers maimed in the wars'. It is still run on lines laid down by the founder and accommodates a Master and twelve brethren.

Lord Leycester's Hospital was the headquarters in the Middle Ages of the Guild of St George the Martyr, then from 1383 of the United Guilds of St George, Holy Trinity and the Virgin Mary.
Guild members were mostly important merchants of the town of Warwick, and governed it in the way the town council does today

In recent years Warwick has almost become linked with Leamington Spa. This town developed as a fashionable spa in Regency and Victorian times, helped by Henry Jephson, a doctor who believed in the curative properties

Jephson Gardens, Leamington Spa

of the local mineral springs. It has some elegant buildings and attractive riverside gardens.

Three miles from Warwick is Kenilworth Castle. Though in ruins, enough of the castle remains to show how strong it must once have been as a medieval fortress.

Kenilworth Castle

John of Gaunt owned the castle in the fourteenth century and in 1563 Queen Elizabeth I gave it to Robert Dudley, Earl of Leicester, who entertained her there in lavish style in 1575. The castle was destroyed by Cromwell.

Stoneleigh Abbey

Not far from Kenilworth, in a well-wooded park, is Stoneleigh Abbey. Originally a Cistercian abbey, it has been owned by the Leigh family since the sixteenth century. The west wing of the mansion was designed by Francis Smith of Warwick in the eighteenth century and contains some fine panelling, plasterwork and furniture. The Royal Agricultural Society now has its permanent home and annual show at Stoneleigh.

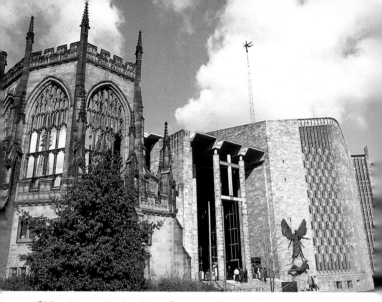

Old and new side by side – Coventry Cathedral

Inside Coventry Cathedral

Going a little further north, Coventry's new cathedral is of great interest. It was built to replace the former Gothic cathedral which was destroyed by German air-raids in 1940.

Epstein's St Michael and the Devil

Designed by Sir Basil Spence, the new cathedral is in a bold modern style, in contrast to the ruins of the old cathedral alongside. It possesses many striking features, not the least of which are the Epstein bronzes of St Michael and the Devil by the main entrance, and the superb tapestry of Christ designed by Graham Sutherland to adorn the chancel.

The altar tapestry by Graham Sutherland

There is also much more to see in Coventry: historical buildings like St Mary's Hall and Bond's Hospital, or the re-built modern city centre with the statue of Lady Godiva standing in Broadgate. Legend has it that she rode naked through the streets as a protest against the local taxes imposed by her husband, Leofric, Earl of Mercia.

The statue of Lady Godiva, Coventry

36

The modern University of Warwick is established on a new campus on the Kenilworth side of the city.

Warwick University

There are numerous other notable places in Shakespeare's Country. Charlecote, three miles from Stratford, is an impressive Elizabethan mansion, the ancestral home of the Lucy family. In the park may be seen a herd of fallow deer and a rare breed of Spanish sheep first introduced in the eighteenth century.

Legend has it that the young Shakespeare was caught poaching deer at Charlecote, and that was why he left home and went to London to embark on his acting and writing career.

Charlecote Park Gatehouse

Charlecote Park, from the terrace. Charlecote has been owned by the Lucy family since the twelfth century, and Queen Elizabeth I was once entertained there on a royal progress in 1572

The Brewhouse

A present-day enactment of the Battle of Edgehill

Leaving Charlecote and passing through Wellesbourne and Kineton the road leads to Edgehill, described by the

Warwickshire poet, Michael Drayton, as the 'loftie Edge'. There is a wonderful view from here.

It is also historic ground, for this is where the Battle of Edgehill between Charles I and Parliament was fought in 1642. A commemorative stone on the roadside between Kineton and Edgehill reminds us of this chapter of English history.

A plaque marks the site of the Battle of Edgehill in 1642

The Oxfordshire border area of Shakespeare Country has much to offer. There is stately Upton House near the top of Sunrising Hill, with its fine collection of paintings and porcelain, not to mention its garden.

Upton House

Sunrising Hill

At Brailes is a very fine church, popularly known as the Cathedral of the Felden or open fieldland; Broughton Castle, home of the Fiennes family, is a moated Tudor mansion.

Inside Brailes Church. There are also some very beautiful stained glass windows to be seen

Broughton Castle from the air

Shipston-on-Stour

Throughout the Shakespeare countryside there are reminders of events which are part of English history. The style of its buildings also reflects the background of

the people who have lived and worked here over the centuries.

A typical example is Shipston-on-Stour on the Stratford to Oxford road, which was a busy market for sheep in Shakespeare's time. The poet's father, John Shakespeare, did business here.

Shipston's name is linked with the River

Tredington

Preston-on-Stour

Stour, a small tributary which joins the Avon just south
of Stratford. Along its valley are the small villages of
Newbold-on-Stour, Tredington, Alderminster,
Honington, Preston-on-Stour and Clifford Chambers,
each with cottages and beautiful country churches
characteristic of Shakespeare Country.

Clifford Chambers

Further towards the Cotswolds, Chipping Campden was one of the chief centres of the wool trade in medieval times. Its magnificent church together with the wool market hall and merchants' houses in the main street show how important it must once have been. Today Campden is generally considered the loveliest of the Cotswold towns.

Chipping Campden

From here the Cotswolds take over from Shakespeare's Country. The small market towns, villages and hamlets are all built in mellowed yellow local stone in the best tradition of English craftsmanship.

Market Hall,
Chipping Campden

Broadway, with its breathtaking view from Fish Hill and Broadway Tower, is perhaps the best known of these places, with Moreton-in-Marsh and Stow-on-the-Wold on the old Roman Fosse Way close runners-up.

Fish Hill Tower,
Broadway

Another town with a speciality of its own is Evesham, which stands on a bend of the River Avon on its way down to Tewkesbury. It is the centre of the Vale of

Blossom in the Vale of Evesham

Evesham fruit and vegetable growing industry. The town has some picturesque old inns, half-timbered buildings such as the Booth Hall, and some splendid Georgian houses. Of its medieval abbey, only the Norman gateway, the churchyard and the fifteenth-century Bell Tower survive.

The Bell Tower, Evesham Abbey

reet in Evesham

Bidford-on-Avon

Between Evesham and Stratford lies a group of pretty villages and hamlets with traditional claims to Shakespearian associations and linked together in the well-known doggerel verse:

> *Piping Pebworth, dancing Marston,*
> *Haunted Hillborough, hungry Grafton,*
> *Dodging Exhall, Papist Wixford,*
> *Beggarly Broom and drunken Bidford.*

These villages are Pebworth, Long Marston, Hillborough, Temple Grafton, Exhall, Wixford, Broom and Bidford-on-Avon. Most of these are still truly country villages, with old-world stone and thatched cottages and colourful gardens.

Cottages at Temple Grafton

The riverside village of Welford-on-Avon, five miles downstream from Stratford, is one of the few places which still has a maypole on the village green. The scattered village streets of Welford are lined with well kept cottages surrounded by gardens and orchard ground. Boat Lane, with its timber and white-washed cottages and colourful flowers, is exceptionally pretty.

And so back to Stratford-upon-Avon once again, with thought-provoking memories of Shakespeare Country, described by Henry James as 'the core and centre of the English world: midmost England, unmitigated English'. Is that true? Shakespeare thought so.

Welford-on-Avon

Index